Big Dog and Little Dog go Sailing

Selina Young

Blue Bananas

First published in Great Britain 2000 by Mammoth
an imprint of Egmont Children's Books Limited
239 Kensington High Street, London W8 6SA.
Published in hardback by Heinemann Library,
a division of Reed Educational and Professional Publishing Limited
by arrangement with Egmont Children's Books Limited.
Text and illustrations copyright © Selina Young 2000
The Author and Illustrator have asserted their moral rights.
Paperback ISBN 0 7497 2809 4
Hardback ISBN 0 431 06984 0
10 9 8 7 6 5 4 3 2
A CIP catalogue record for this title is available from the British Library.
Printed in Dubai.

Big Dog was an inventor.
Some days he invented lots of things
and some days he didn't.

Last Tuesday Little Dog helped
Big Dog make a shiny red boat.
(Just like that!)

Big dog bounced out of bed extra early

and bounded noisily

down

the

stairs.

Little Dog was still snuggled up in bed when Big Dog burst in with the breakfast tray.

Big Dog ate his breakfast and talked excitedly with his mouth full. Today was the day for trying out their new boat.

Little Dog thought this sounded fun

so she got up and washed behind her

ears and put on a clean scarf.

Big Dog made a list of all the things they should take with them.

Little Dog packed all the things into a big basket. She put in her umbrella just in case.

Big Dog made his favourite sandwiches, peanut butter, cheese and jam.

At last they were ready to go.

Big Dog was so excited he raced

out of the door and ran on ahead.

The boat was tied to the jetty.

It bobbed up and down in the water.

Big Dog galloped up the gangplank

and leapt on board.

Big Dog and Little Dog's boat

was made out of lots of

bits and bobs. It had:

A motor for calm days.

A sail for windy days.

A wheel for steering.

A lever for going fast or slow.

A telescope for looking through.

A rope for pulling the anchor in.

Two life jackets.

A cabin with two bunks to sleep in.

A galley with a little cooker,

and three round portholes for looking through.

Big Dog turned the key and the engine
started. Chug splutter chug chug.
Carefully he steered the boat through
the harbour and out to sea.

Then Big Dog pushed the lever to 'Fast'

and off they zoomed. Their ears flapped

as they whizzed along. The boat went

thump thump against the waves.

Big Dog thought that going fast was amazing. Little Dog wasn't so sure. She'd rather be fishing.

Big Dog stopped the boat in a shady

cove and dropped the anchor with a

S P L O S H!

They got out their fishing rods and
Big Dog helped Little Dog put bait
on her hook.

Big Dog and Little Dog threw their

lines out to sea and waited for the fish

to start biting.

It wasn't long before Big Dog felt

a sharp tug. It must be a fish!

He pulled on his line.

It was hard work.

A horrible monster with spikes

came flying out of the water.

The spiky fish pulled itself free and

swam away.

'I don't like fishing any more,' said Big

Dog. 'Let's do something more exciting.'

'Like what?' asked Little Dog.

After that they went snorkelling.

Big Dog took a bag to collect shells.

One, two, three, they jumped into the

water with a big splash.

Snorkelling was fun.

Little Dog liked counting the fish.

Big Dog was busy seeing how many

shells he could fit in his bag.

When Big Dog's bag was full of shells,

they swam back to the boat for some

lunch.

After lunch the sky got darker and a terrible storm began to blow. Big Dog and Little Dog went down below to make some hot chocolate, and warm up.

Big Dog was just pouring the milk into
the mugs when **Bump!** the boat hit
something!

They'd crashed into a big island.

Big Dog dropped the anchor and

Little Dog lowered the gangplank.

Little Dog fetched her umbrella and

Big Dog grabbed his telescope. Then

they ran ashore.

'Let's explore,' said Big Dog. Together
they ran up the hill to the top of the
island. It was very hard work. The
ground was so shiny and slippery.

Don't be silly, that wind has blown all the rain clouds away.
Big Dog

At the top of the island they sat down and took turns to look through the telescope.

Then Big Dog felt rain drops.

Plip plop! Big drops of rain began to fall out of the sky. But there was not a rain cloud in sight. Little Dog put up her umbrella. Splish splash went the rain.

Suddenly there was a big rumble and the island began to shake. It was so bumpy Big Dog and Little Dog fell over and tumbled down the hill.

They jumped aboard their boat and hid
under their bunks.

Just then a big voice said, 'Whoops!

I've bumped into someone's boat.

I hope I didn't tip them out.'

Little Dog peeped out from under the table and saw a big black eye at the porthole. A deep voice said: 'Hello, anyone at home?'

Big Dog and Little Dog came out from their hiding places but all they could see was the island.

'I'm sorry I bumped you,' the voice
continued kindly. 'I always seem to be
bumping into something. Last week it
was the lighthouse and it hurt my nose.'

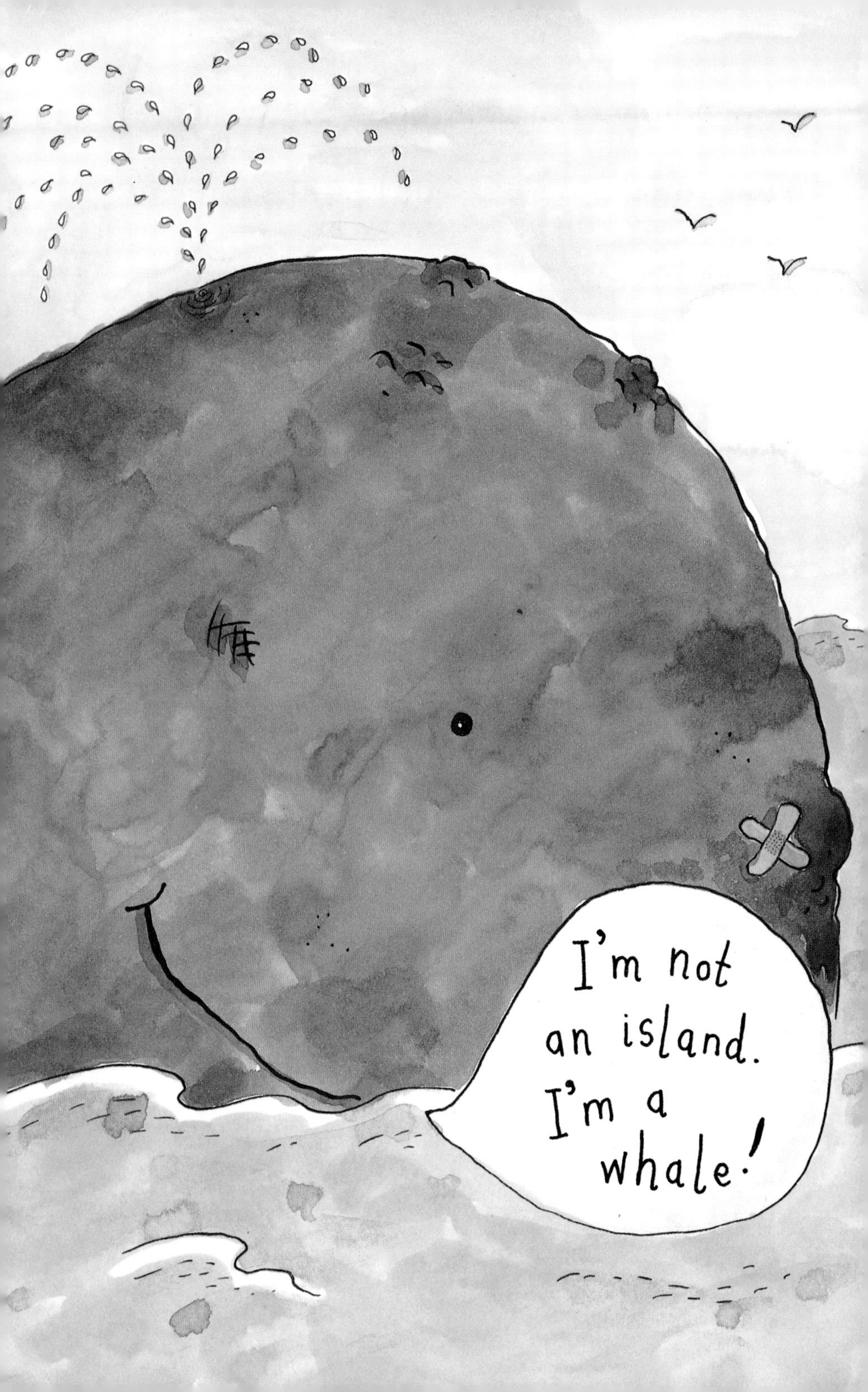
I'm not an island. I'm a whale!

The whale explained how he kept

falling asleep and drifting into things.

He showed Big Dog and Little Dog all

his bumps and bruises.(They were very

sympathetic.)

Little Dog suddenly had an idea.

She whispered into Big Dog's ear.

'Good thinking!' said Big Dog. 'Whale

can have our anchor!'

The whale thought it was such a brilliant

idea he offered Big Dog and Little Dog

a ride home on his back.

What an exciting boat adventure they'd
had. Little Dog helped Big Dog pull the
boat up on the beach. Then they raced
home for tea.

Big Dog cooked some fish fingers.

Little Dog mashed some potatoes.

Then it was time for bed.

Little Dog went to sleep straight away.

But Big Dog was wide awake planning

a very special outing for next weekend.